Waking the World

Author and Illustrator
DOUG ROUTLEDGE

Ambassador International
GREENVILLE, SOUTH CAROLINA & BELFAST, NORTHERN IRELAND

www.ambassador-international.com

Once, not so very long ago, there was a cricket. He lived in a small crack at the baseboard of a young boy's closet. This crack was in the far corner beside the cobweb that hung over a marble and a paper clip. Nearby was something that looked like a chocolate with the cherry eaten out.

This boy's room was in the back and up the stairs of a small house on a little street.
This street was on the outskirts of a tiny little town, far from the big city.

"Noise! Noise! Noise!" is how Rodney Peterson's father described the big city. That was also the reason the boy and his family moved to this little town.

This quiet place might very well have been the perfect place for Rickety Bitick Cricket. You see, "Rick," as his friends called him, had a dream. This is the story of the night Rickety Bitick Cricket woke the world.

Rickety had been thinking about this for a long time. He was known in Cricketdom as the loudest chirper anyone had ever heard. He even worked out every day just so he could be louder.

Now, crickets don't make sounds by yelling like Mrs. Stenger, the gym teacher, does. Oh no. That would be silly. They make their cricketing racket by rubbing their back legs together. Please don't laugh. It's true! This is very serious to a cricket. Crickets make noise in the same way that Oliver Wrinkledorf, the slightly pudgy boy in second grade, did when he walked down the hallway in a pair of corduroy pants.

Oh! Did I mention how Rickety had been working out? He would do leg-ups on blades of grass and leg-downs on small pebbles. He would do hip-hops and hop-hips. He would do quiet chirping and loud racketing. Rickety was a very hard worker.

He also watched for the right time to wake the world. He knew that the stars had to be just right. The day would have to be troublesome so that people would be restless. The night air would have to be light so that the sounds of chirping could carry. Most of all, though ... the most important thing was for there to be quiet all over the earth.

It just so happened that this was that kind of night.

"Perfect," thought Rickety.

Of course, he would not have known how perfect it was indeed. You see, it was an awful day all over the world. The Crown Prince of the Pajama Empire had declared that helping old ladies across the street was now illegal. There were wars breaking out across the country of Bola Bola. The President of the Northern States of Anterica had declared that there was no more candy or ice cream left in the whole country. It was even worse than that.

This was absolutely the best night to wake the whole world. Members of the Woo family in Moo Moo were barely sleeping at all. The Frankoviches from Stevegrad tossed with all of the bad news dancing in their dreams.

In Milonia and Bravonia,
the local people fidgeted
and squigetted and
widgetted as they tried
to sleep.
In Bankirk and Ranstock, folks rolled and snored and mulled over a
rather distressing day.

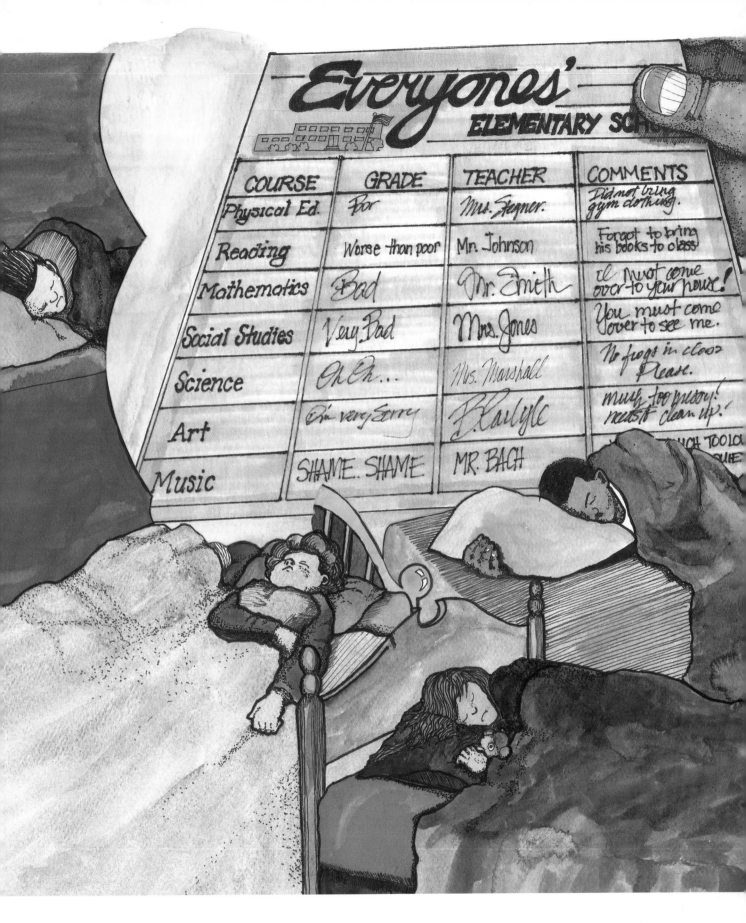

Parents and children alike tossed and turned restlessly all across the earth. Every boy and girl feared the worst. Every mother and father had nightmares all night long. You see, tomorrow, report cards would be sent home.

At midnight, Rickety began to chirp. It was really kind of a warm up. A very soft chirping by most crickets' standards.

"Krickachirp. Krickachirp."

After a good amount of time, Rickety thought, "That's enough. Now to make a little more noise." He began to rub his legs together a little harder.

Well, I guess I don't need to tell you that he began making a tremendous racket, an awful racket, a tremendously loud and awful racket.
"KRICKA CREEKA KRICK A CHIRP!"

Do you know that Rickety wasn't done just yet? It was barely twelve thirty, and Rickety was beginning to feel really good. Why, he reared back, and with all his might, he rubbed, and he rubbed, and he rubbed, and he rubbed. Now, if you didn't know any better, you would swear that you heard five crickets cricking instead of just one.

Well, he "kricked," and he "kreeked," and he "chirped." In fact, and you can just ask any cricket that you see! Rickety made the loudest noise any cricket ever has. Oh my! Other crickets have tried, but they were just regular noise makers compared to Rickety.

Now, can you guess what happened?

Nothing!

Pardon me. I mean almost nothing at all. The Bolarians slept on. The Pajamans all dreamt away. All of the people in Anterica rolled over and cuddled just that much more comfortably.

Moonese and Stevelgradians didn't lose a second of sleep. The Milonians, Bravonians, Bankirkians, and Ranstokians slumbered away like newborn babies, all night long.

After about an hour of this legendary cricketing, Rickety decided that it was time for him to go back to bed too. He was very proud because he just knew that he was the loudest cricket ever.

I know that you're probably asking, "Wasn't he mad that nobody was awake?"

Well, actually, NO. You see, in a small country, in a little town, in a little home at the end of a small road, in a corner bedroom, Rodney Peterson couldn't get any sleep at all.

"Noise, noise, noise," Rodney snorted. "How's a guy supposed to get any sleep around here with all of that loud cricket racket?"

As Rodney Peterson lay in his bed, he thought of ways to change his little town. He could be mayor some day. No! He would be the governor of his whole region, and everyone would have to be nice to each other.

Wait! He could be president, and then he could make the mean people stop being mean.

Well, would you believe that Rodney thought of 6,342 things he could do to make the world a nicer, more loving place? Do you know that one day Rodney became the mayor, and then the governor, and then, the president?

So you see, by waking up one boy who would change the world, Rickety really did wake the world. Now, that made him one very happy cricket.

About the Author

Doug has literally spoken his way across the United States. Every imaginable audience from High School and Middle School Conferences, Colleges, Camps, Educators Conferences, Churches, Leadership and Marriage Conferences.

Doug is known for a hilarious and unique take on relationships, goals and faith. For twenty five years Doug has been, not just "a" favorite speaker but "the" favorite.

What makes him unique is that he presents depth at a life-application level. He can turn the corner from comedy, to tears in a simple phrase.

He and his wife Dawn launched Crossroads Farm in rural Michigan as a training and sending

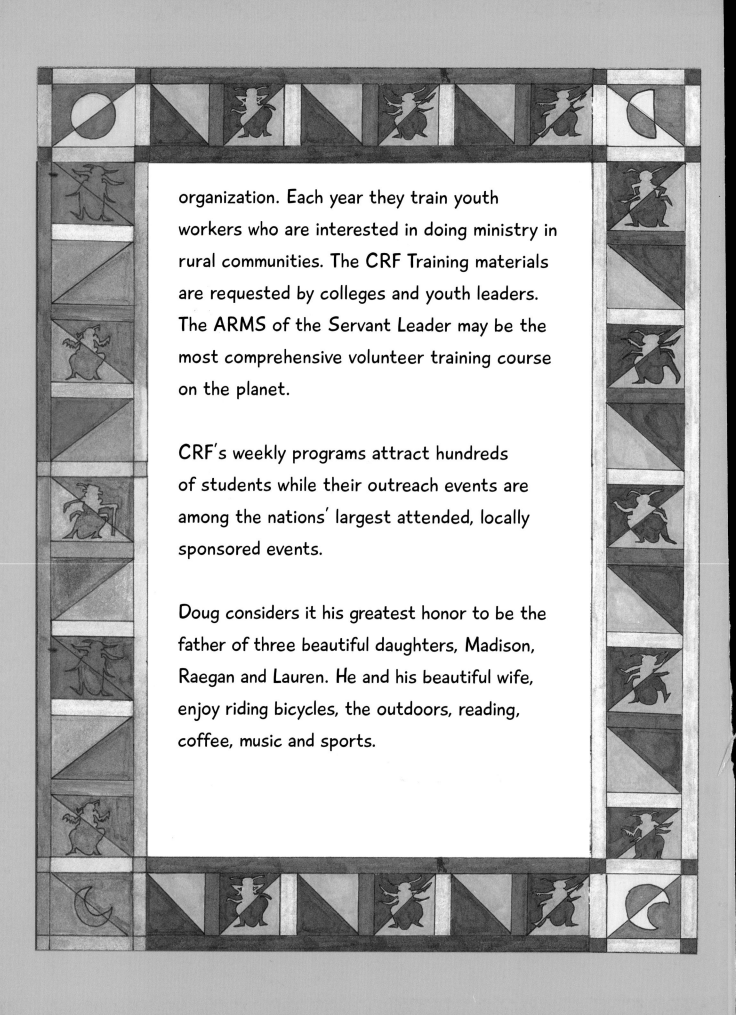

organization. Each year they train youth workers who are interested in doing ministry in rural communities. The CRF Training materials are requested by colleges and youth leaders. The ARMS of the Servant Leader may be the most comprehensive volunteer training course on the planet.

CRF's weekly programs attract hundreds of students while their outreach events are among the nations' largest attended, locally sponsored events.

Doug considers it his greatest honor to be the father of three beautiful daughters, Madison, Raegan and Lauren. He and his beautiful wife, enjoy riding bicycles, the outdoors, reading, coffee, music and sports.